Barbie of Swan Lake

By Mary Man-Kong
From the original screenplay by Cliff Ruby & Elana Lesser
Based on Tchaikovsky's ballet
Illustrated by Joel Spector

 A GOLDEN BOOK • NEW YORK

BARBIE and associated trademarks are owned by and used under license from Mattel, Inc.
Copyright © 2003 Mattel, Inc. All Rights Reserved.
Published in the United States by Golden Books, an imprint of Random House Children's Books,
a division of Random House, Inc., New York, and simultaneously in Canada by Random House
of Canada Limited, Toronto. No part of this book may be reproduced or copied in any form
without permission from the copyright owner. Golden Books, A Golden Book, and the G colophon
are registered trademarks of Random House, Inc.
Library of Congress Control Number: 2003090045   ISBN: 0-375-82639-4
www.goldenbooks.com
Printed in the United States of America   10 9 8 7 6 5 4 3 2 1

Once upon a time, there was a beautiful girl named Odette. She was sweet and kind, but what she wanted most of all was to be brave.

One day, Odette saw something truly amazing—a unicorn! It was being chased by a group of villagers.

"Wait!" Odette called to the villagers. "You'll hurt it."

But the people didn't listen. They wanted to capture the magical creature.

Luckily, the unicorn escaped. Odette followed it deep into the forest. She watched as the unicorn tapped its glowing horn on a rock near a waterfall. Magically, a secret passageway opened, revealing a magnificent lake where fairies and other creatures lived. And they were all talking—including the unicorn!

"Help!" Lila, the unicorn, cried out. The villagers' rope was still tied around her neck.

"Hold still," Odette said. She spotted a crystal in a nearby tree trunk and used its sharp edge to quickly cut Lila's rope.

Suddenly, a beautiful woman appeared. "We've been waiting for you," she said. "I am the Fairy Queen of the Enchanted Forest. And you are the one who has freed the Magic Crystal. You will save our home from the evil Rothbart. He wants to rule the Enchanted Forest and has used his magic to turn people into forest animals."

"You must have me confused with somebody else," Odette said shyly, handing the Magic Crystal to the Fairy Queen. "I'm not brave."

"You're braver than you think," Lila the unicorn said.

"I wish I could help," Odette said, shaking her head. "But I must get back to my family."

Suddenly, an enormous shadow loomed in front of Odette. It was Rothbart! He had seen Odette free the Magic Crystal and knew she would be a threat to him.

Zap! Rothbart aimed his magic ring at Odette and turned her into a swan.

The Fairy Queen quickly placed a crown with the Crystal on Odette's head.

"As long as you wear the Crystal, Rothbart cannot harm you," she said.

Rothbart fired his ring at Odette again, but the Crystal glowed brighter and repelled his magic. Realizing he could do no more evil, Rothbart left.

"What am I going to do?" Odette asked, looking down at her feathery wings and webbed feet. "Can you turn me back into a human?" she asked the Fairy Queen.

But Rothbart had weakened the Fairy Queen's powers. The Fairy Queen changed Odette back into a human, but only from sunset to dawn. During the day, Odette would remain a swan.

"I have to find a way to break this spell," Odette said.

"The secret is in the Book of Forest Lore," said the Fairy Queen. "It is kept safe by a troll named Erasmus."

Odette and Lila the unicorn quickly followed the Fairy Queen's directions and found the Magic Vault, where the troll lived. Erasmus was happy to help them look for the Book of Forest Lore. They searched and searched but couldn't find the book anywhere.

Meanwhile, Rothbart was determined to steal Odette's Magic Crystal.
"Odette is a creature of the Enchanted Forest," his daughter, Odile,
reminded him. "The Magic Crystal can't protect her from a human."

So Rothbart used his evil powers to lure a human to the forest. He turned himself into a bird and led the hunter, Prince Daniel, all the way to Swan Lake. There the prince saw the swan. He was about to shoot her, but he was spellbound by her beauty. Just then the sun began to set, and the swan was transformed back into Odette. Prince Daniel introduced himself, and Odette told him all that had happened.

Enraged that his plan had backfired, Rothbart raised his ring to blast the prince.

"Stop!" Odette yelled.

"You can save him," Rothbart said. "Give me your crown and I will spare him."

"Never," she said. Odette knew that the Crystal in the crown was more powerful than Rothbart.

"Very well," Rothbart said as he fired his ring at Prince Daniel.

Thinking quickly, Odette bravely stepped in front of the prince, and the Magic Crystal protected them both. Rothbart was furious. He left, vowing to get the Crystal somehow.

"Will you show me the Enchanted Forest?" Prince Daniel asked Odette. She gladly agreed, and they strolled hand in hand. The fairies sprinkled their fairy dust on Odette, and her dress turned into a beautiful pink gown. Then they laid out a sumptuous picnic for the couple near Swan Lake. The fairies were so happy that they all began to dance. Odette and the prince joined in the fun.

As the prince danced with Odette, he asked her to go with him to his castle. He wanted to protect her, but Odette would not go. She knew she was needed in the forest to help her friends defeat Rothbart. Prince Daniel agreed to leave without her only after Odette promised to attend the royal ball at the castle the next night.

Later that night, Erasmus ran to Odette and the Fairy Queen. He had found the Book of Forest Lore! Inside, they discovered the spell of the Magic Crystal:

The one who frees the Magic Crystal will share a love so true,
so pure, that it will overcome all. If, however, the true love pledges
love to another, the Magic Crystal will lose its power forever.

Lila and the Fairy Queen told Odette that she must go to the ball and see the prince. After the prince declared his love for her, the spell would be broken.

The Fairy Queen used her powers to change Odette's clothes into a beautiful swan gown and her crown into a sparkling tiara. And the fairies gave her a glittery necklace. Everyone danced around with joy. They couldn't wait for Odette to go to the ball the next day.

Suddenly, Rothbart swooped down from the sky. He kidnapped Erasmus and took him and the Book of Forest Lore back to his dark palace.

"My, my," Rothbart said as he read the book. "I see the Magic Crystal isn't invincible after all."

Rothbart planned to cast a spell on the prince so that he would think Odile was Odette. If Prince Daniel pledged his love to Odile, the Crystal's power would be lost forever.

The next morning, Odette turned back into a swan. She and her friends went to rescue Erasmus from Rothbart's castle. Odette flew into the palace and brought Erasmus back to the Enchanted Forest. Once the troll was safe, Odette flew to the prince's castle.

At the ball, the prince danced with Odile, thinking she was Odette—thanks to Rothbart's evil spell. Odette flew near the castle to warn the prince about Rothbart's plan. But Rothbart saw her and quickly shut all the windows. She was locked out of the castle!

As the prince danced with Odile, he asked her to marry him—still thinking she was Odette. When Rothbart heard this, he asked Prince Daniel, "Do you love her?"

"Yes, I love her with all my heart," said the prince.

As soon as Prince Daniel uttered those words, the glow of the Magic Crystal slowly started to fade, and the Prince saw who Odile really was. Outside, Odette suddenly changed back into her human form and fell to the ground unconscious. Rothbart dashed over and took the Crystal from Odette's tiara—the Magic Crystal was finally his! He put his prize on a chain and wore it around his neck.

The Fairy Queen and her fairies hurried to
bring the injured Odette back to the safety of
the Enchanted Forest. Rothbart chased them,
but the prince followed, and he and Rothbart
engaged in a fierce battle.

"You don't know when to give up, do you?"
Rothbart asked as he raised his magic ring.

At that moment Odette woke up and rushed
to protect the prince. They tried to shield each
other from Rothbart's evil magic. Rothbart just
laughed and zapped them with a bolt from his
ring. Odette and Prince Daniel fell to the
ground, holding hands.

But Odette and the prince's love for each other was so strong and true that the Magic Crystal began to glow brighter than ever. Sparks of lightning shot out of the glowing Crystal and surrounded Rothbart. Soon there was nothing left but the Magic Crystal. Rothbart was gone forever!

"Are you all right?" Odette asked the prince after the spell was broken.

"Yes," said Prince Daniel. "Rothbart tricked me. It's you I love, if you'll have me."

"Oh, yes," Odette said as she threw her arms around the prince.

The Enchanted Forest was saved! Soon there was a huge celebration in honor of Odette and Prince Daniel.

"And you said you weren't brave," said Lila the unicorn.

"A wise unicorn once told me that I was braver than I thought," Odette said with a smile. "And she was right."